The Secret Stealth Bomber

G Parashuram

ISBN 978-93-5610-501-0
© G Parashuram 2022
Published in India 2022 by Pencil

A brand of

One Point Six Technologies Pvt. Ltd.
123, Building J2, Shram Seva Premises,
Wadala Truck Terminal, Wadala (E)
Mumbai 400037, Maharashtra, INDIA
E connect@thepencilapp.com
W www.thepencilapp.com

DISCLAIMER: *This is a work of fiction. Names, characters, places, events and incidents are the products of the author's imagination. The opinions expressed in this book do not seek to reflect the views of the Publisher.*

Author biography

The author is an engineering graduate from Karnataka University and worked as an executive in a defense undertaking of Government of India. Later he worked in private industries and also as a faculty in several institutions. One of his works titled "The ISI agent and other stories"" is also published on several platforms and this is the second work to be published.

CONTENTS

The scientist, the prey

Sekhar is a middle aged engineer in the organization. He joined as entry level Scientist B and promoted only once in ten years of service and presently assigned the design of power amplifier of counter measures of the Stealth aircraft. He is forced to report to the project manager who was his junior but superseded him three years later. Though extremely hard working and brilliant he was passed over many times for promotions so that his juniors have become his equals and some have become his bosses too.. The peculiar trait of avoiding The Director on his rounds made him lose on promotions. He is made to stagnate in the present post for more than seven years where as everyone moves to higher scale within five years. He is from military background with his father a JCO in the army.

His dad was an instructor in training center and one recruit died in his platoon. It was attributed to the brutal treatment he gave the recruit during one training session but court marshal cleared him of the charges. He was exonerated but yet transferred from training center to regular army unit. Sekhar particularly remembers the annual quarter inspection by the Commanding Officer which was terribly hard on his mother. The military wives have an informal network which shares the gossip about the CO regardless of the language barrier. Thus Malaya lees, Punjabis, Marathas and everyone else shares bits of gossip with sign language and broken Hindi. One particular CO was notorious for roving eye and rumored to indulge in bottom pinching of wives of young soldiers. He particularly remembers the stratification of wives of army personnel. Wives of officers are called mem sahibs, of JCOs as dharma patnis and of NCO and other ranks as aurat meaning women.

His mother is in military parlance is just another 'woman'. That is ok for him but what is galling is the CO laying his hand on his mother's shoulders while his dad stood at ramrod attention. Later he came to know that it was his way of signaling for offering commission for her husband and if the lady is interested, the matter shall be pursued further. It was a perfectly voluntary affair and no coercion is involved. The women folk used whisper something like Harjeet commission which he understood to be victory after defeat commission. Har means defeat and jeet means victory in Hindi. Later he came to know that it is a code for getting a permanent commission as officers for their husbands if they are willing to visit the guest house just for one night. The CO being an honorable man would certainly keep his word and many wives have gone the extra mile for the promotion of their husbands to commissioned rank.

When he joined the organization as a fresher from college, he was full of drive and enthusiasm firmly believing that the country can take on any super power with its huge base of skilled manpower and industry. As the days wore on, he got a different picture when every component has to conform to certain MIL STD of the USA. Only components certified to be MIL standard compliant should be used and the traceability has to be perfect for acceptance by the customer. MIL STD for this test or procedure as per some MIL STD.

Then he realized that the media is painting a different version from the reality. We cannot afford to antagonize the sole super power. The thoroughness of documentation and procedures was astonishing and he realized that we are nowhere nearer to their level notwithstanding the tall claims made by politicians. Every component is MIL certified and all design is based on their components. In contrast the Russian systems might be crude and lack sophistication but they solve the same problem in a simpler way. Their level of transistor integration is very low with few transistors to any IC but they achieve the goal finally with their own components. No fancy microprocessors and no VLSI in their systemS but achieve the objective in a simpler way. He had never seen any western parts in their systems and the reliability of Russian systems is legendary. He respects their fierce spirit of national pride in matching whatever the western countries launch in the field. In case the lone super power decides to bring down the defense production, an embargo is enough to do it. Only commercial considerations keep the business going and they don't see the need to block low tech exports.

Then he recalled the feeble attempts to attack US 7th fleet aircraft carrier USS Enterprise with Kamikaze attacks by volunteers from Air force during 1971 war. There was no effective deterrence to such threats and only astute and superb military leadership brought the war to an end in a short time. India must be ever grateful to it's military personnel for eliminating the dagger on her eastern flank.

But the gains of that victory were frittered away with meek handing over of 93000 POWs without any strategic gain. Now the Chinese are coming due the short sightedness of political leadership of that time. Both father and daughter had successfully destroyed any strategic gain and we are back to square one.

His dad was in 62 and 71 war and it is heart breaking to recall the pain of their loved ones back home about thoughts of horrors they might be facing in the battle field. What if their father, son, husband or brother walks into an ambush of the enemy? He recalls the fate of Capt Saurab Kalia and his patrol when they walked into the ambush of the Pakis. He recalls their torture for 21 days before being mercifully shot to death. He imagines his father in that situation and that thought sometimes makes him unable to sleep.

Then he remembers The Highway Of Death during the Gulf war where coalition forces simply picked targets just like in a video game and destroyed thousands of vehicles of all types along a 80 kilometer stretch and wonder if our forces can survive in such situations. The more he thought about such situations, the more depressed he became.

Sekhar became anarchist at heart abhorring all types of authority and delusional.. Somewhere he read that as per the study of juvenile delinquents there were three important traits in the childhood of future criminals. They were bed wetting, cruelty towards animals and propensity to start fires. He had killed hundreds of birds, rabbits, rats and bandicoots with his air rifle. He particularly hates dogs when they start barking not withstanding their obedient and docile nature at other times. A dogs bark has all the odd and even harmonics and designed to irritate. Once a dog start barking, he will search for a nearby stone or stick to chase it away. Such is the pathological hatred for barking dogs.

He was also notorious for bed wetting well into his teens due to the constant beatings from his father which used to return as nightmares in his sleep. The only last redeeming trait not starting of fires which he never indulged and this he believes has kept him out of Borstal school.

The predator

ACP Seenappa hails from Chittoor district and rumor has it that he is related to the highest political power in the state. He was a very ambitious person. As soon as he graduated from the academy as sub inspector of police, he was advised by his mentors to get posted in agency area to make a pile of money.

So his first posting was in Chintapalli where he put his talents to best use. Due to its remote location and no road connectivity, it was eminently suitable for ganja cultivation and favorite posting place for the department. He mastered the business of ganja trade and was well versed in all of its nuances. He was mentored by the seniors about all the nuances of the trade; exactly the places where it is planted in the remote hilly areas and its volume. The route of transportation and the couriers were all he was trained and plunged himself into the trade extracting good commission. He made a pile of money. For cosmetic purposes he would intercept some consignments and pose with media for publicity warning the traders before hand to be on safe side. They too played the game well forfeiting small consignments to keep everyone happy. It all looked good on his service record and due to his untiring effort in stamping out the illicit ganja trade, he was promoted as CI. There was a general crackdown on drugs monitored from center after one investigative journalist ran a series of articles on national news channels .Special teams surveyed the difficult terrain with drones and identified huge fields where ganja was being cultivated. Earth moving machinery was brought and the entire crop was uprooted and burnt down.

 His mentors advised Seenappa to lie low for some time till dust settles down and in the interim he was promoted for his untiring efforts in fighting the ganja mafia. After promotion, he moved to the city as SHO of a police station. Apart from usual collections, he was desperately looking for new sources of income. He came in touch with loan collection executives' who have fallen on hard times due to strictures of courts consequent to a suicide of one defaulter. Due to that incident some loan collection executives were arrested and thrown into jail. Then a brilliant idea took shape in his mind.

He would call these executives one by one and got the list of defaulters and their addresses and stuck a deal. The jurisdictions doesn't matter, his father in law would take care of it.

His modus operandi was simple. He would call the defaulter and make him visit his station. The locality and jurisdiction doesn't matter. Once inside, he would strip the defaulter naked and hang him upside down. Then the beatings would start but carefully not to kill the victim as that would make it a lockup death which would go CBI. Third degree treatment is an art and only trained professionals can do it without killing the suspect. Every police station has some specialists among the staff specializing in that method. For the same reason some amateur officer in their enthusiasm have taken up third degree treatment on their own resulting in death of the suspect. In that case even his father in law cannot bail him out. The family members of the defaulters would wail, scream and beg the CI to spare the husband, father or brother whatever the case may be. The CI would work out a deal to get the money from their relatives, friends or loans from anywhere to let defaulter go free. Until the money is paid, the beatings would continue.

In case the defaulter doesn't visit the police station, the CI has another trick up his sleeve. That is call up the defaulter and inform that one of his relative had come to the city and met with an accident He would advice the defaulter to visit his police station for more details. Some gullible ones have fallen into this trap and once inside, the recovery treatment would start.

Life was good for our Seenappa as he made another pile with 'solving' dozens of cases and he was looking for more cases. Then the unthinkable happened. This case was big one involving a big industrialist and the amount was in millions. So Seenappa zeroed in on this appetizing prey and after collecting the details from the recovery agent, he went to the place on the other side of the city. He confronted the industrialist and was bringing him to his police station in his jeep. While bringing the family members called up the Chief Secretary who happened to be the brother in law of the industrialist. So even before reaching his precinct, the CS was waiting.

He went to the case details and enquired about registration if any of FIR, procedures as per CrPC and jurisdiction. Seenappa tried to browbeat the CS in his usual arrogant style and that was when CS reached for the Chief Minister. One terse communication and the Seenappa had his tail between his legs. The CS insisted on moving this pest from regular law enforcement and Seenappa was shunted out to ATF, Anti Terrorism Force.

The chaos

Sukumaran Nair was from Ex Air force retired as Master Warrant Officer (MWO) highly experienced gentleman. His grasp of the intricate technical issues was phenomenal and was posted in Customer Service Department as service engineer. He is a good friend of Chandrasekhar and drops in at his department whenever he is at head office. They share some small talk.

Sekhar: "Where have you been Nair?"

Nair: "You know the issue with Tail Warning Radar?'

Sekhar:" Yes I have heard about it. What was it about?"

The Russian Bomber project was a limited one of 120 numbers. For political expediency, it was split into three places, on part at Hyderabad, other part at Badarpur where the two are integrated and final installation in the bomber at Nagpur. During flight trials the radar used to work erratically triggering an alarm in the tail warning system. Then it will be sent back to Hyderabad for rectification and repair where no fault was observed usually. Every radar make three trips to three different locations before installation but the issue of false triggering persisted. Air force could not accept aircraft with erratic tail warning radars. That was when Nair was put on special assignment.

He went over there and saw dozen radars lying on the test bench. He opened every one and began thorough physical inspection. All were identical and then he opened the Russian prototype for comparison. Upon thorough physical inspection, it was found that all production models have one tiny one microfarad capacitor missing. Due to this missing component, the radar was giving a false alarm from the tail warning section. They procured the missing component installed and tested which was successful. The radars were mounted on the aircraft and all flights were successful with no false alarm from the TWR. He got appreciation letter from the General Manager and returned to head office. All this he narrated to Sekhar.

Sekhar asked "What about the precision approach radar?"

Nair" You mean the Czechkoslavian one?"

Sekhar "No, not the old one but new one at Goa."

Nair: "You know our wing commander turned Chairman was a flight lieutlant in 65 war. He shat in his flying suit when chased by a Paki saber jet. On time scale he went up to Wing Commander but could not go higher in spite of power of The Clan. They could not crack the steel frame of defense establishment and so he opted out of service and was offered a manager's job in this defence public sector undertaking. Then The Clan promoted him every year till he reached grade 10 in as many years. After some study trips to US and UK ostensibly to look out for collaboration projects, he took over as Chairman. But he did not forget his buddies from his academy days. His friend Challoo was offered the indigenization of the perfectly working Chekoslavian radar. Our project manager Challo who never held a soldering iron or a screw driver in his life, became the chief designer of 500 kilo watt precision approach radar. His team made many trips to Goa for assembly and testing of this Radar. Every one made huge pile of money in the form of TA and DA. Some people purchased flats some open plots with that money but the Radar would not work. After several years and many more TA bills, finally it was made to work but it was not all weather radar. It won't work in the rainy season.

Sekhar: "What is the status now?'

Nair" The air force doesn't want it and refusing to take delivery. They have stopped coming for inspection altogether."

"Then what is going to happen?"

"They knew that our wing commander turned chairman is 59 years now and next year he is going to retire. News is floating around that he is trying for the post of ambassador to USA or UK but all I can guess is he will be offered post of ambassador to Somalia at the best. The Clan is powerless against another steel frame. Once he retires, they will junk the radar kissing goodbye to 100 crores of public money. They all fucked up the Chekoslavian Radar."

Nair also said that Challo is also due for retirement next year and nobody going to look after the white elephant after that. He also made some trips to Goa but the task is gigantic and cannot be undertaken by a single person. So he also dropped out citing his inability to service the radar with erratic documentation and nightmare of logistics.

Nair asked" You know the HF 24 Marut aircraft?"

Sekhar said" Yes I heard it was our own best designed plane at that time." Nair said" It was the worst one for servicing as the engine has to be dismantled for servicing the Gattling gun. It was a nightmare. Thankfully simpler MiG 21 was procured and we junked those planes.

Nair went on" Last month I went to Vizag for the harbor trial of our naval version of VHF tranceiver. Forget harbor, it was not working on the test bench itself."

Sekhar said "You mean it was not getting switched on?"

"No, it was switching on alright. The Captain made me use two of our own units, one as transmitter and the other as receiver. And he told me to call the receiver on 143 MHz which I did. Then he made me tune the receiver all over the band. The signal was breaking through on all frequencies of the VHF band. He adviced me to take both the units, throw them into the sea and go home peacefully. I was utterly ashamed and reported to the DGM."

Sekhar asked "What happened next."

Nair said they are still working on it and that is the latest situation. If it was successful therewould have been a huge order for those systems.

It was time for lunch break and they left for the canteen. After Sekhar returned to his table, he froze in shock. The radar manual volume 7 which he left on the table before going for lunch was missing. He frantically searched the table and all the drawers but couldn't locate it. Then he went through the shelves and cupboard but it was nowhere. He remembered the private electrical contractor undertaking some repairs to the power lines and he remembers one person in particular as a suspicious character.

The customer rep was coming for inspection and he could not afford to delay any further. Off he went to publications section and got one more copy even without signing up for it. But he knew a fifth column is operating and it seemed that they all hail from one particular state. He didn't want to inform anyone not to further complicate matters and kept quiet. He was planning to get out of this dead end job to migrate to some western country including the Gulf. Why involve in a deadly investigation before leaving was his stand , so he kept quiet. Once an enquiry starts, he might never get out of it.

The wing commander and the union

As he was waiting for the customer rep, an ambulance went past their building with sreaming sirens. Everyone rushed to the windows to see who might be the sick person. His assistant Raju also went outsiide to get some information and came back after the ambulance left for the hospital. What he narrated sent him into depressive mood.

Wing commander Chopra was on deputation and posted in the R&D division. One day he parked his car outside the shopping complex and went in for shopping. By the time he returned, someone was inside the car and he didn't know how that thief gained access to a locked car. One boy was fiddling with the stereo inside the car and playing at full volume. He got enraged at the utter disregard for someone's property and pulled him out. As he came out, he gave him a tight slap. That boy fell down and ran away towards the worker's quarter. The officer cheeked inside the car for any missing item but it seemed nothing was missing. He started the car and went to his department.

It seems the vandal's dad was a worker in the Stores department and a close friend of the union leader. That boy went crying to his home and called up his dad. He came home and after listening to the story went to the shopping complex to make enquiries. There he came to know that it was Wing commander Chopra of R&D division who slapped his beloved vandal. Along with two of his friends, they went to the medical center and barged into the Chief Medical Officer's cabin. They insisted on examining the boy and issue a medical report on the injuries caused by that officer. The CMO examined but could not find any grievous injury.

He asked the workers "What report do You want?"

They said "Write that blood is coming from the ears of this boy."

The doctor said "I don't see any blood." and gave some first aid. But he refused to be cowed down and sent them away.

The next day, the gang came to the floor of the R&D division where Wing commander Chopra was working and cordoned off the entire floor sending every one away to ground floor. Then they barged into his cabin and started beating with their fists and standing on his table, kicked him with their legs all the while shouting obscenities about his wife, mother and daughter.. As he was profusely bleeding he fell down unconscious in his seat. The beatings continued till they felt satisfied and left leisurely. Someone from his department called for ambulance and took him away to the hospital. He was hospitalized for two weeks and not turned up for work afterwards.

After some weeks, Nair came to his office and Sekhar enquired about Wing commander Chopra. It seems he went to his commanding officer who called up the GM who didn't do anything. He wrote to the HQ who promised to look into the matter but nothing happened. Then he wrote to The Supreme Commander of the Armed Forces who referred the matter to his Commanding Officer and that is where it ended. Finally he cancelled his deputation and went back to his unit. The GM doesn't want any issues with thr union which may throw the organisation into turmoil with labor unrest and he alone shall be held accountable.

Nair asked "What would you do in case you are in his boots?"

Sekhar said" I will wait patiently till I get eligibility for pension and then resign. Once I am out I will act on my own without leaving a trace and get all of them one by one like Amitabh in the movie 'Aakhri Rasta.'

Nair asked " Do you know what happened during Assam Blockade/"

Sekhar said" I know it was a prolonged sieze with blocking all movements."

Nair "One commissioned officer with his wife was reporting to the base. They were waylaid on their way and were stripped naked and his wife was molested for many days. After they were released from captivity, Government wanted to take action. The head of their organization warned that Assam shall go up in flames if anybody is taken into custody for that crime. That is where the matter ended. "

Nair said" During the blockade we were starving as all supply routes were closed. We foraged the mountains for wild bananas and fed ourselves until supplies were air dropped. The lives of soldiers are never easy as shown in movies and even their families are subjected to untold hardships. Many such incidents never make it to the mainstream media."

Nair went on" You know my dad was also from Air force and was in 62 war. Due to pathetic crying of Nehru, Kennedy dispatched his air force to help our defense forces. My dad was at Hindon base and one Hercules transport aircraft of USAF was about to take off. One airman was on ground duty marshalling the C130 and as it was taxing on the tarmac, the airman who my dad remembered as a black, somehow was caught in the propellers and within seconds was pulverized by the gigantic blades. When the pilot saw it, he switched off the engines came down to the tarmac, knelt down on the ground and raised his hands to heaven praying for forgiveness. The airman's body was never found but only bits and pieces of his flesh were seen on the surrounding buildings. It was a poignant situation and whenever my dad recalls that scene his eyes would be filled with tears."

The assassins

O thou Delight of Men, Janardana?
By overthrow of houses perisheth
Their sweet continuous household piety,
And-rites neglected, piety extinct--
Enters impiety upon that home;
Its women grow unwomaned, whence there spring
Mad passions, and the mingling-up of castes,
Sending a Hell-ward road that family,
And whoso wrought its doom by wicked wrath.
Nay, and the souls of honoured ancestors
Fall from their place of peace, being bereft

The
Song Celestial.
or
Bhagavad-Gita
(From the Mahabharata)

Being a Discourse Between Arjuna,
Prince of India, and the Supreme Being
Under the Form of Krishna

Translated from the Sanskrit Text
by

Sir Edwin Arnold,
M.A., K.C.I.E., C.S.I.

New York
Truslove, Hanson & Comba, Ltd.
67 Fifth Avenue

Bhagavad Gita Verses 1:41 to 1:43

Tata Chari is he head of a secret organization like KKK of USA. While KKK uses the usual direct Yankee methods of guns and bombs, this organization uses more secretive truly Asian way of eliminating the enemy. This group believes the British while ruling the country for close to 200 years have stolen secrets from the ancient texts of the country which explains their rapid industrialization and growth. For example the Wright brothers copied the airplane design of our own Talawade and so became the pioneers of heavier than air flight in the world. But the rise of the lowly classes must be kept under check to reclaim the lost glory of the country.

With the newly found liberty and jobs guaranteed in the constitution framed by thei demigod, they are rapidly moving up the social ladder in the cities. But back in their villages they are restricted to their ghettos in dalit hamlets. They might have become police officers and collectors in cities but in their native villages, they are not allowed to settle among higher castes. In the cities, they are freely mixing with other castes and some are also marrying females of higher castes as exactly lamented by Arjun in the epic poem Bhagavad Gita in Mahabharat. Back in their village they were burnt alive in haystacks for having affairs with the females of higher castes. Things are exactly turning out as feared by the great warrior on the battle field of Kurukshetra.

The aim of this group is to thwart the raise of lower castes by secret and deadly methods. With prevailing civil rights laws where calling the lower castes by their caste names itself a cognizable offence, they have perfected a system where the victim is dispatched to nether worlds without any violence or proof. All that required is the victim's horoscope which the group draws basing on the time and place of birth. They have a mole in HRD who provides these details. For other dignitaries, the information is available in public domain. Their successful hits include Seetha Ram of Dalit party who was showing great promise of becoming leader of opposition and from there when tables turn might become tough contender to the throne in some distant future. And Shiva Yogi the upcoming politicians from Amalapuram. His father was a domestic help in Tatachari's agricultural fields and were born under servitude to their family since several generations. Such low life becoming prime minister and defiling high caste females is beyond the imagination of his community. They successfully eliminated him in a helicopter crash and it was brilliant in its execution. Some cases where the details are not correct, the attempt ends in a near miss. In most cases success is assured as they don't perform rigorous rituals and known to take bath once in five days. "Which god can save these stinking vermin?" is the logic of this group.

In the place of work they have also scored some successes in eliminating Chief Manager Prakash Rao who died of some mysterious illness at the age of 45 Rajaram from Purchase at the age of 40 years and four others. Presently they are working on Ramadass, Chief Manager Quality Control.

Ramadass was a crypto Christian despite being a devout Hindu. After birth of his daughter one worker showed extreme interest in her, raising suspicions in Ramadass mind as to his motives. She was born very fair and almost looked like Eurasian. This Apparao from his department used to visit his place under any possible pretext. In her fifth year she became terribly sick and Ramadass had taken her to many specialists. No doctor could diagnosis her illness as she would not eat anything and if fed forcefully, would vomit it. Then it was the turn of spiritual solutions and he visited many temples and pilgrimage centers.

The one Christian friend suggested that he visit a small chapel near his home which he did. As they were waiting outside in the open ground for the service to begin, suddenly a shower of blood fell on his daughter. He was terrified and looked around and saw no one and above him was a clear sky. No bird was flying over the chapel and no animal was seen anywhere near the vicinity of the chapel.

When the father prayed and sprinkled holy water, he saw a black snake come out of her which threatened the preacher not to come near to her. The preacher anyway sprinkled holy water on her and saw the black snake burning to ashes. She became unconscious and fell to the ground. After several minutes, she woke up and recalled seeing a golden light in which a figure sat in a golden throne and spoke to her. She didn't remember what was told but she became slowly ok. One wound came up on her right heel the preacher said it is exit wound of the black snake. It took one month to heal after that she became healthy. This experience made Ramadass a devout worshipper of Mother Mary and used to wake up at one o'clock in the night to light a candle to recite the rosary as told by the preacher. He used marvel at the incident of sprinkling of blood from the sky on his daughter and started attending the chapel on Sundays but avoided mega churches. He did not wish to get into trouble as he got job on reservation quota.

In his department there was one Catholic employee from a place called Soroda in Orissa state. He invited to visit his place where a festival of Mother Mary takes place on 11th of February every year. Legend says about a century ago French missionaries established a church in the remote jungles of that state where even roads were nonexistent. They used to travel by horseback and were running schools and hospitals in the remotest parts among tribals. One such church was established at a village called Dantilingi about seven kilometers beyond Soroda..

As per folklore, a terrible epidemic was sweeping around that place hundred years ago and many were succumbing to it due to absence of medicare. Then one day one old lady came down from the nearby hillock and advised them to partake the water from the spring from the hillock. Miraculously a fresh water spring appeared from the top of the hillock on 11th February and the water healed all of them from the epidemic. Every year when prayer service is held on that day water used to gush from the spring after the service is over. Nowadays the spring has almost died out and water rarely comes out. Some years there used to be no holy water at all.

Anyway when Ramadass visited that place, there were about one lakh people camping in the open with insufficient toilet services. Many were made to do in the open as the organizers could not plan toilets for such massive population which gathers for only three days of year. Ramadass was provided accommodation in a friend's place and after prayer his friend managed to get few spoonfuls of holy water from the spring which was muddy. Getting that water itself was a blessing as the previous year no water was available from the spring.

Ramadass returned to the city by train after the pilgrimage and placed at the altar the plastic bottle containing the spoonful of holy water. As usual, he woke up at one'o clock in the night to light a candle. As soon as he stuck a match, his daughter woke up in terror screaming. He lighted the candle and asked her "What is the matter?". She answered that she had witnessed a terrible scene in a vision.

Next day morning there was terrible screams and wailings in the neighbor's house. Two brothers with their wives were staying in that house. The younger one had a deep attachment towards his elder brother and his wife whom he looks up as almost a mother. After getting married the younger one's wife demanded separation which was unthinkable to her husband. Fights were a regular occurrence and on that particular day the wife threatened him with dowry harassment case. Substantial gold and cash with proof was given as dowry. The husband got terrified, went into bedroom, latched the door and hanged himself to death with a bed sheet.

Then Ramadass daughter recalled her vision. When he stuck the match to light the candle, she saw an enormous black human about nine feet in height riding and an equally huge bison over their house, threw a noose onto their house. The spoonful of holy water from the spring diverted the noose from their home and fell on the neighbor's house and saved them from death. Ramadass idly wondered who might be interested in killing him or his family members. He wondered since how many days this Hindu God of Death, Lord Yamaraj was hovering over his home. The spoonful of muddy water from Dantilingi ended his mission in a disastrous way for someone else instead of his family who were the real targets.

The Monthly review meeting More chaos.

The monthly review meeting started at 10 am as scheduled. First it was the turn of Digital Computer Frame of Tupelov Bomber. GM asked the Chief Manager of the project Ramakrishna rao.

"What is the status of these units?"

The head replied that all of 10 units were lying with quality control pending inspection. GM looked at Ramadass in a quizzical way fully knowing that they must had solid reason for holding up.

Ramadass replied "Sir, they all failed in high voltage test at 5 kilo volts."

Ramakrihna Rao said "Sir this is a low voltage device operating at maximum 110 volts and question of applying 5000 volts doesn't arise anytime."

Ramadass answered "Sir, if someone certifies to that effect, we shall submit the same to the customer with endorsement."

There was a deadly silence. How could anyone overrule the original designer without a sound technical reason?

Finally it emerged that the assembly manager had consumed original wires meant for 110 sets in making 70 sets only and they had a shortfall for the balance 40 sets. The Chief Manager instructed his assistants to scout for the wire in the scrap yard and they could locate some old wires. Only issue was that the stock belonged to the radars of 1965 vintage and had deteriorated. Insulation had become weak resulting in breakdown and sparking at high voltages.

Ramadass persisted "Sir, if anyone certifies that the item is not exposed to high voltage and is used for low flying aircraft, we will clear them today itself."

GM thought long and hard. This Ramadass is a hard nut to crack. The original purpose of posting SC candidates in Quality Control is that they are technically dim and also they are also docile. Having entered the service with low marks, they can be easily shouted down. The GM made a mental note to write adverse remarks on Ramadass in the quarterly secret assessment report on SC and ST executives and move him to Stores later.

Next on the agenda was control panel for Analogue Computer.

GM wanted to about the latest position. The concerned shop manager replied that 10 numbers were rejected by quality control.

Again Ramadass was ready" The cable form behind the panel is bulky due to extra length taken up by the technicians and after fixing with fasteners the solder joints are snapping. This is a workmanship issue and we have explained to the assembly executive for corrective action."

The turn of R&D department and the General Manager wanted to know the status of the ongoing Naval Version of Transceiver.

The R&D chief replied the project is in limbo after the resignation of four members of that group. It was a great setback for the project as they could not find replacement engineers to take forward the project.

Next came the large scale failure of VHF transceivers during testing. Rmadass explained "Sir, the assembly operators are mounting wrong components on the pcbs."

GM asked "Why so?"

"Sir, the soldering technicians are not using spectacles and so assembling wrong components with wrong color codes."

GM innocently asked "Why don't they use spectacles."

Ramadass replied "It seems it affects their glamour and makes them look old."

At this everyone started laughing. GM asked "OK, but how the boards passed inspection?"

Ramadass replied "Since assembly operators were not wearing spects why should our ladies wear them and look old. That is the stalemate and we don't know how to resolve this issue."

Again one more round of laughter.

The QC chief added that he has put some executives to physically double check the boards before mounting and take corrective action.

The Contact

It is time for annual promotions and expectedly, Sekhar's name was not in the list. He too was not surprised given his aloofness with the bosses and inability to make small talk. Every morning, he will attend the meeting and after giving the status report, walks out of the Chief Manager's office where as others hang around for coffee and usual small talk. He will answer to the point making no room for further talk. He knows others might be gossiping behind his back but doesn't care. The message he doesn't like his boss and the boss being a human, reciprocates his feelings not liking him inspite of his wonderful work. So again he was passed over and he felt it is time to look for jobs outside the country. First he has to procure a passport and so went to the passport office.

There he saw one lady pestering everybody for something. The security guard told her to get out and not to bother the officers. He became curious and enquires about her. The guard told him the brief history of that lady.

She was married off as a third wife to a foreigner and went to Gulf. She begot a son and became an object of hatred and jealousy to other wives. She returned to India after some years with her husband. To kindle jealousy she became coquettish and started flirting with her relatives.

Her husband really became furious and one day took his son on the pretext of shopping and left India with her passport also. They realized late in the night that he had left India. Being illiterate and poor they did not know what to do. She was making many trips to passport office trying to get another passport.

After listening to her story, Sekhar felt very sorry and met her. He introduced himself and promised to help her. He got her phone number promising to visit her place next Sunday. He gave her five hundred rupees towards expenses and returned to his place.

Back at his work place, Sekhar found himself thinking about her all the time. Somehow the week came to an end and he made himself ready for the rendezvous. He took out his old Chetak and started for old city, to the address given by the lady he met in passport office. On the way he purchased some fruits and slowly made his way to the old city. Enquiring the directions he made many turnarounds and finally reached her place. It was a predominantly a slum and he felt curious eyes following his movements. Unknown to him, it was crawling with spies of all sorts. He found her place, met her parents and brother gave them the fruits. He asked for the copy of old passport to pursue the matter further at the passport office. It was shown to him and he copied it on his mobile phone. They offered him lunch which he partook and it was almost evening when he started return journey.

On the way, he was stopped by traffic cops to verify his documents. All his papers of his scooter were in order including the driver's license and his own documents. Then they let him go.

It was almost night when he reached his place as the total distance came to about 40 kilometers and with the traffic jams it took him two hours to reach home.

The week started as usual and he returned from work made supper, watched TV and studied his hobby project of vacuum tube radio receiver. He found on intermediate amplifier of the Russsian Radar interesting and trying to use it in his FM radio receiver. He needs some components and wanted purchase them in the city some day.

One evening after work he left for the city to buy components for his project and one old lady met him at the shop and advised not to venture into the city for some time. She said "You are in great danger." Then she vanished in the crowds. Surprised, he came back home and after supper went to bed.

At two o clock in the night, the stray dog outside his house started barking violently. He woke up and saw some shadowy figures moving in the bushes opposite his home. It was a lonely figure sitting in the bushes and he thought someone defecating in the bushes. He woke up and switched off light and waited. The person also waited for nearly one hour then he felt whoever was sitting in the bushes must be enjoying the company of mosquitoes and that is his funeral. He ignored and went to sleep; the dog also went on growling all night.

He was attending to work in the factory busy all day. At night he went to bed and again the shadowy figure has moved to his window sill grouping around for something. Next day he saw his watch missing and some circuit diagrams missing. When he woke in the middle of the night, he could smell tobacco smoke meaning whoever hiding in the bushes was smoking. So next day he brought choicest cigarettes as offering and kept on the window sill and went back to sleep. Morning the packet was gone and he ignored that shadowy figure.

The surveillance was intensified with a group accosting him in the market place and strange phone calls in the middle of the night. Slowly he began to notice a pattern. Whenever a phone call comes from an untraceable number, something dreadful might have taken place. There was a bank robbery in the city where the robbers did not leave a trace and for some nights random calls were coming to his phone. Same with a train derailment and he felt they are trying to pick up what is called 'chatter' from him his phone. He was flattered for having been credited with such organizational skills. He stopped calling the lady in old city and made no effort to meet her or attend to her passport issue.

Then a miracle happened. At two in the night there was a lady in white standing on air high above in a corner of his bed room. She said " Do not fear , and don't react or make fun of them. I am taking care of you."

He woke up terrified and wondered about meaning of that vision.

One particular incident made him recall the intensity of surveillance. He used to go for walk and buy newspaper while returning. One day as usual he went for walk and while returning instead of turning into his street, he went straight towards the laundry where he had given clothes for ironing and wanted to collect them. He turned into the laundry lane and stopped at the first house which is the laundry. The laundry lady went inside to get his clothes and suddenly two persons, one on a scooter and other on a motorbike swooped down on him and about to say something, May be it was like "you are under arrest" or something to that effect. Then the lady came out of her home with a bag containing his ironed clothes. On seeing the woman and the bag, the two suddenly mounted their two wheelers and fled. Sekhar was flabbergasted and wondered at the intensity of their surveillance. He didn't know why they are doing it and how long they are monitoring his movements. The purpose of it all was a mystery to him. He marveled at their persistence but realized it like was a huge dinosaur with million eyes and ears but with a small brain. They are good at gathering information but have limited ability to process that it. Why would anyone in his right mind wait till daybreak for passing secret documents when he had all the night to do so? Then he remembered the goddess's warning about not mocking them and so ignored the incident. They also have a hard time ensuring the safety and security of the citizens what with abundant supply of fifth columnists. He really empathized with their plight.

. There seems to be a desperate bid to link up with some of the events and trying to pick up chatter whenever such incidents take place. Before National Festivals like

Republic Day and Independence strangers used to follow him in the market place keenly observing his movements. It looked like they were expecting him to plant something in crowded places and he wondered why would he do it.

The marriage of Elizabeth

Next day at work Srinivas the technician from antenna testing unit came to him with a gate pass. He was going out after lunch to the city for showing Zoo Park to his in-laws along with his two kids, While signing it, Sekhar enquired about wife and kids. Srinivas replied" The eldest son is studying in first standard and the second,a daughter is in UKG. Their mother Elizabeth also coming along and she also appeared with a gate pass. He signed it and wished them a happy day.

Ten years ago they were fresh from their polytechnics and school as Lisa was only a matriculate. They were posted to his section. Srinivas was from Kakinada and Lisa as she is called by friends, from Ernakulam. Right from the day she joined, Lisa had fallen head over heels in love with Srinivas and used to spend long hours in front of his seat. So much so that her work was pending and was reprimanded several times. But slowly every one took for granted their so called 'affair 'but surprisingly they were not seen outside. Srinivas avoided all contact with her outside the factory and whatever 'affair' she had with him was one-sided. Everyone including the HOD sympathized with her as the proverb says "Every one loves a lover" but wondered how two individuals with seemingly diverse backgrounds could make it to the wedlock. Srinvas was orthodox vegetarian and Lisa die- hard non vegetarian and yet was ready to follow his dietary preferences. But Srinivas was terrified even to discuss his plight with his parents.

Lisa started reporting sick and applied leave. She was complaining about nausea and once went to wash room for vomiting. Then she didn't report to duty for three days. All females in the department started staring at him and passing snide remarks as a wolf in sheeps's clothing and such things. The more forthright male workers started congratulating him for becoming a father. He was utterly shocked and confused and wondered what that was all about. What did he do to become a father? The cacophony reached a crescendo and he was getting scared day by day. If parents come to know about this calumny, they will definitely kill themselves. So he decided to go back to his native place never to return.

The train to Kakinada from Secunderabad starts at 6 AM, so Srinivas decide to leave by that even without reservation. He planned to leave home by 4AM and make it to the railway station somehow. Some early morning buses might be there or by auto and money was no problem. Once he reached his home, someone would come and get his belongings.

He was awake all night and at four in the morning, came out of his with just one bag. As soon he locked his room, huge crowd from the neighborhood pounced on him shouting obscenities. He saw females from his department with their relatives ganged up shouting things like "Cheat, criminal" etc. He was scared and didn't know what to do.

Then he was made to open his room and locked up with some burly males standing guard.

Slowly a huge crowd gathered outside his room and they were told that he was running away after making a girl pregnant. They all wanted to beat him but Lisa's friends restrained. Then a band appeared with a pundit and hurriedly arrangements for a wedding. Then Lisa appeared demure and shy befitting her role as a bride. They brought a golden mangalasutra and he was made to tie it on her neck. In the evening reception was held in a prominent hotel where guests from his department were served sumptuous dinner all at the expense of the bride and her relatives.

Slowly the news trickled to Srinivas's parents and they vowed never to see his face in their life time. After one year when the first child, a son was born, the grand parents came with gifts and grand ma imparted her wisdom to her daughter in law in taking care of the new born. After the birth of the second child, this time a girl, everything was forgotten and there were regular visits from both sides.

Srinivas also used to take eggs sometimes and not averse to wife eating her preferred dishes. In that respect he showed great tolerance in not enforcing his preferences and gave her freedom in bringing up the children. Finally it all ended up well.

The big meeting

The defense minister Chote Lal was flying over to review the progress of all important projects. He was known for his tricks of survival under many dispensations sitting on the fence when the situation doesn't suit him and jumping into winning side at the right time .He survived many raids by different agencies and reached present position after lot of horse trading, wheeling and dealings. The venue was the conference hall and many high powered dignitaries were present. One Air Marshall was attending alongwith high powered civil servants empowered to take decisions of highest order.

At the outset the minister welcomed the gathering and in shudh hindi began ranting about the state of affairs in the field of defence reasearch. He asked the official representing that department.

"What is the status of the Bheeshma engine?"

Godbole, the artful dodger replied "Sir it was sent to Russia for high altitude test"

Minister asked "What happened to that test?"

Godbole replied "It might have passed or might have not passed sir."

Minister: "Bakwas bundh karo" meaning cut the bullshit "Give me a straight answer, did it passed or not?"

There was a pin drop silence.

Finally the secretary cleared his throat and said" Sir it developed only 60 kilonewtons at high altitude of 10 ten thousand feet. At sea level it developed 80 kilonewtons."

The minister started ranting about the dismal performance of the engine. "You fellows have spent a lifetime feeding off this project. You acquired doctorates, went abroad on study tours made lot of money and after thirty years this is what you come up with this junk. I shall send all of you to jail on charges of treason if you do not come up with a solution."

The scientific advisor sent a slip to his assistant which reads as "What is the weight of staplers recovered from the ashes when the ED raided his farm house.10Kgs, 15 Kgs or 19 Kgs?. Tick the right answer."

His assistant ticked 10 Kgs.

The officer corrected him and sent the slip with no 19 Kgs.

They were discussing the case of misappropriation of the gentleman in the fertilizer scam . When the ED raided his premises he made a bonfire with the currency notes to destroy evidence. There were five hundred rupees notes stapled together with thick stapler pins and all that the raiders recovered was the pins with the currency notes burnt to ashes. Then they collected the pins and the total weight of the recovered stapler pins came to 19 Kgs. They could not arrive at the correct amount and so he was let off due to benefit of doubt. So here he was reincarnated as defence minister after much horse trading and deft manovering.

He asked the Air Marshal" What is the present situation of your squadrons?"

He replied "Sir, we have only 28 squadrons ready against the sanctioned of 46 squadrons".

Chote lal asked them "Do you realize what it means? If our enemies decide to wage a war, we are left with half the sanctioned strength to fight a two front war. If things get rough, we might have to go for missiles due to the reduced strength of our Air force. The repercussions cannot be predicted now. You people have let down our country badly."

Again the minister wanted to know the status of imported engine.

The secretary explained that they are developing a thrust of 100 Kilo Newton with a mean time between failures of 1000 hours.

He asked what the status of the dozen imported engines .

'Sir, we wanted to reverse engineer the engine and so even cut open one to that end, but we could not proceed further due to the limitations of metallurgy as we do not know the exact composition of the parts. They are closely guarded secrets and they would not share them at any cost."

"What is the so called MTBF of our Bheeshma engine?" the minister wanted to know.

There was a deafening silence.

The secretary meekly replied "About 10 hours."

Minister said " Ok then complete the program of 84 aircraft with the imported engines. Our external affairs ministry shall proceed with negotiations and we shall sanction required funds."

It was the turn of secretary. "Sir, our airframe was designed for Bheeshma engine. The intakes are optimized for our own engines. With the imported engines the aircraft develops only 80 percent of its maximum thrust."

The minister was furious "What is the solution? He screamed.

The secretary cleared his throat" The intakes have to be redesigned to match with the imported engine."

"What is the time frame for that modification?", the minister wanted to know.

After few minutes of heavy silence, the voice of the Project Director came out" Five years".

Chote Lal lost his cool." After thirty years of playing around, you rascals want another five years. I know this five years shall stretch to another ten years. You get those engines and start producing those planes right now."

The Air Marshall was depressed as he realized our boys shall be sent into battle with under powered aircraft and the outcome in any dogfight is a foregone conclusion.

Meanwhile Chote Lal had one more brainwave. He said "Since you say our engine develops only 80 Kilo Newtons, you mount two of our own engines to make up thrust of 160 Kilo Newtons and design an invisible stealth bomber. The entire world must marvel at the ingenuity of scientists and engineers. We shall make all parts here itself and make it 100 percent indigenous."

The Project Director interrupted." Sir, do you mean all parts like landing gear and ejection seat also?.

Minister replied "Yes that is exactly what I had in mind. You assign a group to the landing gear and ejection seat and make them report progress to me personally . And I make it abundantly clear that no resignations shall be accepted. Anyone resigning shall be arrested under defense rules and jailed."

The minister instructed his PA to circulate the minutes of the meeting and left in a huff.

After the minister left, hurriedly they formed design groups for landing gear and ejection seat for the invisible stealth bomber.

Then quietly imported the two items and gave them to the two groups.

Ramamohana rao was made head of ejection seat department.

Ramamohan had joined after passing a tough written exam and equally tough viva. In his batch of 1500 candidates, 200 candidates were shortlisted and everyone was sent feelers to pay 5 lakhs to get the appointment offer letter. He could have pursued MS in USA like his friends but the precarious financial situation of his parents prevented that possibility. So they sold the last one acre of agricultural land and paid the bribe. In hindsight he regretted by not opting the software route which might not have resulted in such a life and death struggle.

They studied the imported seat and went about reverse engineer that item. After several months and many reminders from the minister's office they came up with one an identical one. It was supposed to be certified in a static test and during testing there was some mismatch in the synchronizing. The canopy did not eject at the expected time and the pilot's head hit it crushing his skull.

Later Ramamohana rao committed suicide in his home hanging himself from the ceiling.

There were many more suicides in that establishment in another two years.

The final solution

The profile of Sekhar landed on the table of ACP Seenappa. He thoroughly studied it and came to a conclusion. Here is a brilliant engineer obviously a loner and not member of any powerful group. He was seen visiting a slum in old city and must be having an affair with someone. There were secret photos taken while moving in that part of the city and also getting in and out of that house. Some technical documents were also obtained by the operatives. This must be an open and shut case of espionage and it is a too tempting a reward to be passed on. Though he made his fortune in many dubious ways, recognition is what any one craves. A beautiful combination of honey trap, espionage and treason is exactly the ingredient for a spy thriller and he shall be the hero who cracked the case. Whenever he thinks of the medals and awards, he gets excited and feels aroused. Due to his proximity to the power center, it is presumed that he is eminently suitable to do the honors.So the predastor was waiting for the opportune time.

Sekhar was invited for the wedding of one Chief Manager's daughter at Srisailam some 200 kilometers from Hyderabad. At first he did not wish to go but later changed his mind and joined the wedding party. They hired a bus for fifty of them and it was a pleasant journey through Nallamal forests of Andhra Pradesh.

They reached the temple after passing over the hydroelectric project and the dam. As they were getting down, Sekhar stayed back as he had no intention of going to the temple but rather walk around the place. Arrangements for the marriage were being made and as he was loitering, one middle aged lady in saffron came to him and said " I made you come to this place."

He didn't understand the propose of that message and as he turned around, she was gone.Later he joined the marriage party and had the feast and went back to the restroom. Some commotion was seen among people and he sensed something happened somewhere. Then the worker Narayana from his department met him and passed information that there were multiple bomb blasts in the city and several places. Slowlynews was trickling down about the series of blasts.

Though no one from the wedding party or their kith and kin were affected in the series of explosions, the mood was somber among them. They returned next day to the city after taking many circuitous routes as some areas were cordoned off blocking the traffic.

After reaching the city, Sekhar took an auto to home and switched on the TV. The ride back home was tiresome with slow moving traffic due to many detours and the city was swarming with cops of all types. All channels were full of the gory details of the bomb blasts and the aftermath. Pieces of human flesh and some limbs with burnt clothes were shown repeatedly making him depressed .He switched off the TV and went to sleep.

. Next morning he went to work and groups of workers were gathered here and there discussing the news. Someone's relative was also one of the victims. Rumors were floating thick about some more impending blasts. Sekhar was left pondering about the mysterious lady and her secret message. How did she know about this before hand to move him out of the city at the exact moment? Why didn't she prevent this if she knew about it well in advance?

He was utterly confused and decided to divert his mind to something constructive like his pet electronics projects. So he went for shopping to the city for buying some components and took a bus as it is convenient to return home in the evening rush hour traffic. As he was waiting at the bus stop, a Toyota Innova car stopped in front of him. Two burly persons in their 30s got out of the car and one person shoved him into the back seat. The other got into the seat on the other side. He was too stunned to react and it took him several minutes to realize whatever was happening to him.

When he came back to his senses he shouted at them in Telugu."Who are you? What do you want?"

They didn't bother to answer and after repeated shouting one of them told him to shut up. Then he took his phone out of his pocket, and they snatched it back from him. One of them said "Our sir will explain everything and soon you will be back home."Then they took out a black mask and covered his head and he did not where they were heading. He could hear the noise of the traffic and he could make it that they were right in the middle of the city by the volume of the traffic.

After an hour or so it looked like they have reached a big building as he could hear gates being slid open and someone checking the car's papers. Then the car was parked and they pulled him out with his shopping bag. He was conducted to a lift and after reaching the top they took him to a hall like area and removed his blindfold. He opened his eyes and could make out that it is the Control room right in the middle of the city. It must be of five or six floors he could not recollect as he saw it many times on the way to the city shopping malls. From there the noise of the traffic down below was faint and the place was realtively silent with severals decibels below the street noise.

 Then he saw the verandah barricaded with heavy metal grill. Then he realized the gravity of his situation as the floor is used for interrogating high ranking criminals and terrorists as the screams could not be heard by anyone down below. The grill also has a story of it's own.

A military doctor from the city got posted in the north right after graduation. As he was a bachelor, many pretty young girls were attracted to him. He fell in love with one pretty one and got married without intimating his parents back home. It was a simple affair and solemnized in the presence of the CO and friends in the unit. Everyone was happy for some time but the doctor kept his marriage a secret from his parents. They were on the lookout for a suitable bride for him and finally settled for one among their own caste with a huge dowry. The news was conveyed to him and was told to visit his home in the city for finalization.

Devil entered the doctor's mind and he hatched a plan. He told his new wife that they are going on leave to meet his parents and get their blessings. She was very happy to meet the in-laws and they made reservations for the journey. Meanwhile the doctor put his plan into action and with his medical knowledge silently killed her. The he procured a steel trunk just sufficient for her small size and skillfully dismembered the body. He packed the body leaving no trace of any organic matter and cleaned his residence. He boarded the train with the trunk and reached Hyderabad.

Once he reached the city he did not contact his parents but booked a room in a tree star hotel carrying the steel trunk. In the evening he used to go the tank bund a favorite tourist spot in the city carrying a body part small enough to be carried by hand but covered in news paper. At a suitable isolated location, he used to throw that part into the lake.

He went on doing this for several days as getting rid of a human body in small parts is a huge and tedious task. One day he picked up a right hand up to the shoulder, wrapped it in news paper and went for strolling on the tank bund. After doing the deed,he came back to the hotel and slept off. The dismembered hand instead of sinking to the bottom of the lake was floating in the water and somehow reached the bank of the lake. A stray dog picked up the part to feast and sat down on the bank to feast on it. Some passersby noticed the hand and threw stones at the dog to scare it away and called the police. Police came and took the hand into their custody after conducting panchanama.

The hand was submitted to the police doctor for examination. After examining, the doctor gave his opinion that that hand belonged to a young female of 23 years of age and the dissection of it was done by a doctor.

After intense investigations somehow police zeroed in on the military doctor staying at the hotel. He was brought to the same floor in the building and sensing that his fate is sealed; he pushed away his escorts and plunged to his death from the balcony which was open at that time with no grills. The cops got wiser after that event and fitted the balcony with strong grill to prevent recurrence of such situation.

Sekhar surveyed the situation but could not understand how it is all relevant to him. He must been very high up the hierarchy of the criminal kingdom to be given this royal treatment of presidential suite. He was made to sit on a chair near a big table and facing his seat was another chair. It seems a familiar set up for interrogation and somewhere there must be a one way mirror. Two armed guards were keeping a watch over him. There was a lockup with a attached toilet. One guard asked him Telugu whether he would like to have coffee or tea. He thought why not this game to the logical end and asked for coffee. Sometime later a cup of coffee was brought to the table and he sensed some sort of canteen must be there as the building was housing many offices. He drank the coffee and pondered about his situation.

He was not perturbed in the least as he knew someone more powerful was watching over him which was abundantly clear from the repeated messages he received from an unknown source. Once she warned him not to mock them and she would handle them. True they were also living and working under tremendous pressure not knowing from where the next attack would arise.

Then entered Seenappa ACP and took his seat facing him. Sekhar was puzzled and wanted to know who s that person why was brought there.

Seenappa replied in Telugu" I am Seenappa, ACP Counter terrorism" and then asked "How is Ravi Kiran?'

Sekhar was puzzled who the person this Ravi Kiran as there were some engineers and technicians he knew with that name. He asked "Who is that RaviKiran?"

Seenappa replied "Dr RaviKiran your mama (maternal uncle)"

Then he remembered about one of his maternal uncles who went to medical college to study MBBS when he was in fifth standard and even he passed out of engineering college, this uncle was still in medical college even after thirty years.

He replied "I met him twenty five years ago. I heard he got married while still in college and begot two girl children. Finally he got his degree and started practicing getting paid in vegetables in lieu of cash. That was what I heard about him. It seems he was also practicing alternative medicine like acupuncture."

Seenappa asked "Did you know that he was a member of Radical student's wing?"

Sekhar replied " We all know about that. He ruined his own sister who went on sending him money all these years neglecting her own children and they could not study beyond matriculation because their mom could not afford the fees. Her children have migrated to the city and doing menial jobs for survival. Now his father in law is taking care of his children. He is a famous parasite. That is what Chairman Mao done to his family"

Sekhar recalled the attempts of the Chinese to spread their Cultural Revolution back in the sixties. Indoctrination camps were held in secret locations to spread terror by starting fires in the hamlets by sticking phosphorous in roofs of thatched huts. Phosphorous rods bound in wet rags were stuck in the roofs and on becoming dry; the phosphorous spontaneously ignites starting fires. Huts going up in flames were a regular occurrence in those days.

Next in the syllabus was debunking of Indian Mythology and classes were held mocking how Hanuman jumped over ocean to reach Lanka to find Sita, on how a person like Ravan could walk around with 10 heads and so on and so forth. The State cracked down ruthlessly and crushed with terrible force. Hundreds of misguided college students were killed in fake encounters and many familie's lost their bright young kids in the brutal repression of the State. Both the State and Gods fought the existencial threat and the imported Cultural Revolution fizzleed out. It was rightly prophesied by Vallabhai Patel that a Peasant

Revolution of the Chinese variety cannot be replicated in India.

Ravi Kiran was not killed as he confined himself to spread the Gospel of Chairman Mao to all and sundry instead of taking up the gun. Even in police custody he was found preaching to police escorts the Good News of Cultural Revolution.He became what is called an ideologue and used to go around villages preaching how Chairman Mao undertook the Long March in very hazardous circumstances. Chairman Man became their Chairman and so he is worthy of worship.

So our arm chair revolutionary was in and out of jail many times and missed his classes and exams. Many times he went underground to avoid preventive detention whenever something flares up. His course stretched to 25 years bankrupting his sister's family and later his father in law also.

When he recounted the known history of his maternal uncle, Seenappa interrupted him saying in Telugu"We all know about it but tell me where the bombs are."

Sekhar was amused and asked "What bombs?"

Seenappa continued" It was very clever 0f you in fact I would say brilliant to create a cast iron alibi"

Sekhar replied "What is this all about?"

Seenappa: "Very clever to mastermind bomb blasts from a remote location but having a cast iron alibi at the same time."

Sekhar thought that this person has an IQ of a Cretin. He asked him "What makes you think that I am somehow connected to the blasts?"

Seenapa: "We know all about your lover in old city" and dumped some photos on the table. They were taken while he was speaking to her at the passport office. Some were taken while he was on the road on his scooter in the old city and some while he was coming out of Nasreen's house: that was her name as he remembered now. Then the ACP produced coup de grace: a circuit diagram copy on a white sheet, and asked "What about this secret document you were planning to send to our enemies?"

Sekhar looked at the diagram which was a photocopy version of the missing paper from his window sill several months ago. He replied "That is a diagram of IF amplifier of radar receiver and I was trying to modify for FM radio receiver. It is of no use to any one."

Seenappa: "So you were trying to keep in touch with your handlers abroad!"

Sekhar replied" My friend , the operating frequency is around 100Mega hertz and the waves travel in a straight line and so the range is limited to around 60 kilometers as they cannot bend around the curavture of the earth. How could I contact someone around the world? I could have made a HF system if that was the case."

Seenappa said "You were planning to flee the country and join some terrorist organization. They offered you twice your present salary if you decide to join them apart from special bonus after every successful mission."

Sekhar was stunned and after sometime burst out laughing. Seenappa also joined him.

Sekhar:"You have chosen a wrong profession. With your creativity you would have become a great movie writer.

Seenappa became furious and stood up to leave. "We shall discuss further tomorrow." and instructed the guards to send whatever he demands for supper. He was provided with a short towel so as to not hang himself and toiletries... He was locked up and vegetarian meals were brought to the cell. There was a hard slab for a bed and a pot of water. A mosquito coil was also provided and Sekhar was thankful for their thoughtful gesture. He partook the dinner and the guard came to remove the plates. He stretched out on the slab for sleep and the time was 9 pm.

He had fitful sleep and would wake up the every one hour to get up and walk around. He wondered about the motive for his incarceration and believed he shall be set free in the morning. Aroun four in the morning he went sleep and when he woke up it was already six in the morning. He went to the bathe room took bath and wore the same clothes and the underwear started to stink. After reaching home he must take bath again and change into fresh underwear, he thought.

Then the ACP came in crisp uniform and told the guards to get a rope which they broght. He told Sekhar to undress to his underwear which he reluctantly complied. Then he hung him up from two hooks in the ceiling in a configuration where his hands are tied behind his back and ropes were pulled from the hooks. This is the famous treatment called 'The aero plane' treatment and the victim feels his shoulder bones are pulled off from the sockets and the pain unbearable. The ACP took a baton to start beating the prisoner. Sekhar let out a horrible shriek and one guard came running to the cell with a mobile phone.

He said to the ACP, " Sir, the chief minister on the line " in Telugu. Then Sekhar was released from the Aeroplane mode. Seenappa rushed out to speak on phone and came back. He told the guards, "I will come in the evening "then went away.

The ropes were removed from his hands and clothes were returned. He put on his clothes and went back to the slab to lie down. On guard gave a tumbler of water which he hastily gulped down. After locking him up, they went away. After some time they came back with plate of poories and coffee which he hungrily ate up.

Then he fell asleep on the slab. The noise of traffic was become a faint roar when he woke up and it was mid afternoon. He remembered the message of the unknown lady not to venture into the city alone. He ignored it as he did not see any reason to be afraid of anyone." Why should I fear anyone as I didn't commit any criminal act?" was his thought. Then he tried to recollect some of the messages. His phone was confiscated and there is no way of contacting any friend or relative. They must have felt his absence but no way of contacting him. They might have thought he might have taken a sudden trip to somewhere. May be after some days they might try to find him.

He was hungry but no food was provided till evening. Then Seenappa turned up and ordered the guards to bring him out. They opened the cell and after he put on his footwear, put the same black bag over his head. He was taken to the lift which went down as he sensed it.

He sensed the lift was in the cellar which might have been a parking lot. One vehicle was brought to them and he was unceremoniously pushed in. He sensed that he must be in the back seat wedged between two burly persons. Then the vehicle started with the ACP in the front seat.

The vehicle was moving slowly as it was the evening rush hour and it seems the driver quickly got out of the city limits due to several short cuts as he sensed less traffic He sensed they might on a state highway as the speed was more with many heavy vehicles plying on the road.

Then there was silence on the road and it was bumpy ride and he felt the car moving on a dirt road. After some fifteen minutes on this road, the car came to a stop. Everyone got out and Sekhar was pushed out of the car.

They took out the clothe bag from his head and it seemed it was around 8 or 9 in the evening. The lights from the vehicles plying on the highway were faint flickers.

The ACP was in his uniform with the 9mm automatic in the holster. Other cops were in battle fatigues armed with SLRs and he sensed that they have put up a charade for an encounter. The ACP took out a paper stolen from the window sill several months back and gave him to hold it.

He was moved to about twenty five yards towards a tree and made to face them. Then the ACP called the two other cops with SLRs to load their weapons . There was no response and the two cops simply stood there not uttering a word. Seenappa became furious and shouted"You mother fuckers! Don't you hear what I am telling you" in Deccani. The other cops were in sullen silence and were looking down.

The ACP came to them and shouted "Don't know who I am? I will kick you out of the force. I will send you on punishment to CRPF. You know I can do that. Now load the rifles and get ready." In Deccani.

One of them said "Sir, we have been in many battles and seen our friends cut down in a hail of bullets in combing operations. We have never killed a unarmed civilian in our line of duty and we shall never do it."

The ACP got furious and said " you say unarmed? Now get this" and went to the vehicle. He came out with a tapancha made in northern states available for two thousand rupees. He opened the barrel and shoved one round into the bore and threw it near Sekhar.

"Now this fellow is not unarmed" and ordered them to load the SLRs.

They were looking down in sullen silence.The ACP shouted,"Alright, I will do it myself." And pulled out the 9mm automatic from the holster. He turned the safety catch off andcocked the gun.

He pointed the 9mm at Sekhar and pulled the trigger. Instead of a powerful explosion, there was a muted noise with no flash from the barrel end. Sekhar understood that it was a squib load and wished to warn the cop but kept quiet Without checking his weapon, the cop pulled the trigger agaien and the gun exploded in his face.

Shards of metal tore into his face and some pieces got into his eyes also into hishead. Blood was oozing from his head and the escort party was terrified He collapsed on to ground

.

There was complete silence and the other cops were too stunned to react. Then one of them came to his senses and called someone from his phone. They checked his pulse and realized he is dead. They sat down on the grass and waited.

After one hour several vehicles came to the spot and it was nearly midnight.

One high ranking officer wearing epaulettes equivalents to a brigadier came in his staff car and surveyed the scene. He was muttering" Good riddance, I warned this bastard many times and the problem has gone away by itself."

He called Sekhar and told" Go away in our car and I warn you not to discuss today's incident with anyone." He gave one five hundred note from his purse and called someone."Drop him near his home or wherever convenient for him. And give back his mobile."

He was told to get into one car and someone returned his phone. It was a long ride back to the city and he told them to drop off at an all night eatery in the city. He got down had a breakfast of poories and tea. Then he called an auto rickshaw and reached home.

He opened the door and flopped onto his bed.

Next morning he got ready to attend work after shaving and wearing clean clothes. He turned on the TV for news and saw a video about how a breave cop fell to the bullets of terrorists in the jungles of Nallamalla. Special bulletins of the encounter were being aired on all channels. He turned off the TV and left for work.

He punched in and reached his department. As soon as he took his seat, he was sent for to meet the HOD who never liked him.

As he was still standing, the boss growled at him and asked" Where you had ben without giving any intimation?" Sekhar replied that he was called to his native village due to medical siuation of his grandmother and being a remote location he could call on his phone.

He sat down in his seat and turned on the computer. Then Nair came and sat down in front of him."Had a nice time?"

Sekhar gave a short grunt by way of answer. Then Nair said" Do you know Dr Seshadri of special materials division went missing for last three days?"

Sekhar answered "No" , then "what happened to him?"

Dr Seshadri was a brilliant scientist did his doctorate from foreign university in Radar absorbing materials. The science behind that technology was a closely guarded secret and very few nations have access to it. Recently Dr Seshadri visited US to see his son doing MS and returned last month.

Nair went on "His car was parked by the road side near railway track and body was found mutilated by the side of tracks last evening"

Sekhar was left pondering about Dr Seshadri. Here was a person who had everything in life: power, prestige and wealth but chose to end his life in such horrible way. In the labs everyone was discussing the death of the scientist. Sekhar was checking his personal mail and found one about a job interview he attended about a month back for and academic post. He sent an acceptance letter even thoughthe salary was very less. Working time is fixed and as the college was located in the outskirts of the city, the bus journey takes one and half our one way. So he had to spend three hours every day in bus which promptly leave the college at 3.30 in the evening.

He sent the acceptance letter and also submitted his resignation letter requesting expedite relief from his post. The boss called ffor him and it looked like he was actually happy to see Sekhar go away. He was queried about the atatus of his project which had come to final stage after passing low temperature test at minus suxty degress and also high temperature test. High altitude test was also successful and his reliever only had to take over from a advantageous position as all design issues were sorted out successfully. He was given one month notice period to leave the job.

He came back to his seat and then his friend Krishna Rao from material division came to meet him. After exchanging pleasantries, the topic gyrated to Dr Seshadri and what was whispered was shocking to Sekhar. It seems Dr Seshadri was on a spying mission to procure Radar Absorbing paint and successfully sent on sample back before leaving to the country. Feds got wind of it and raised Cain to get him behind bars. They made it official and sent warrant for his extradition. The usual time frame is 30 days to execute that warrant but somehow it was stretced beyond that. Pressure was building up on him to give himself up. Once in their custody, the resident Bubba would be delighted to have an exotic asian customer and his fate would be sealed. So he sought and obtained the final solution on railway tracks. That was the end of the brilliant scientist.